PAUL BUNYAN

by Sydnie Meltzer Kleinhenz
illustrated by Mark Weber

Harcourt

Orlando   Boston   Dallas   Chicago   San Diego

Visit The Learning Site!

www.harcourtschool.com

Paul Bunyan was born in Maine. He was so big, his cradle was put in the ocean. The waves rocked him to sleep. One day, he kicked too much. The sea crashed over the town.

Everyone said Paul had to go.

So Paul grew up in the woods. He could beat deer in races. He could play with wild beasts and tame them. He snacked in orchards, eating apples as if they were gumdrops. As a young man, he became a lumberjack.

Once Paul found a baby ox in the
snow. He warmed the ox, but it stayed
blue. Babe the Blue Ox ate heaps of
hay and turnips and grew fast. He
outgrew his barn in one night! Babe
was strong and a big help to Paul.

One day Paul got a letter from the king of Sweden.

Dear Mr. Bunyan,

Some people from my country want to live in North Dakota. Can you clear the trees there in one month? Thank you.

The King of Sweden

Paul hired many loggers to clear the land for the king. To feed them all, he made soup in a nearby lake.

The hot soup made fog form. It was so thick the loggers had to chop it to see their food. Paul and his loggers

cleared the trees, and the farmers
came.

The king wrote again. He said, "My
farmers cannot grow crops on land
with tree stumps."

Paul pounded each stump into the
ground so the farmers were happy.

Paul and Babe headed to Maine to visit Mom and Pop Bunyan. Rain had soaked the ground and their feet sank into the mud. Their footprints filled with rain and became the Great Lakes.

At home Paul asked, "What's new?"

Pop said, "I hear the President needs help. He's digging a ditch so people will know if they are in the United States or Canada."

Paul and Babe helped. That ditch became the Saint Lawrence River.

Pioneers kept moving west. Paul and
his loggers cleared the frontier. They
came to a place with good, dark dirt.
"This looks like a fine spot to grow
things," Paul said.

"Is there water?" someone asked.

Paul swung his ax into the ground.
A hot, wet gusher shot into the sky.
"Plenty!" he yelled, as they all ran.

That gusher still shoots up today in
Yellowstone Park.

Paul and his loggers hiked on hot sand to reach the west coast. Paul felt so weak, he dragged his ax. It dug the Grand Canyon.

"I won't survive this heat," a man said.

Paul had to think fast. He got a load of corn and let the hot sun pop it. The popcorn snow made everyone feel cool. The loggers put on mittens and played. Soon, they were ready to start hiking again.

Summer is a hot time of year for a hike. The sweaty loggers spotted a river and cheered as they ran to it. Babe, too, had a huge thirst.

Babe drank and drank. The loggers bent lower to drink. Babe drank more, and they began to worry. Just as they feared, Babe drank that river dry!

Paul Bunyan slapped his thigh and chuckled. Then he led his loggers into the woods. They still had plenty of work to do on the frontier.